The Very Tough,

Very Old,

Old Lady

ELLIE MCDONAGH

DEDICATION

To my classmates in St. Joseph's, for always loving Francis.

You're the reason this book is here, so thank you and I hope you enjoy!

Any relation to any person, living or
dead, in this book is completely
coincidental. This story is a figment
of the author's imagination.

First published Oct. 2023

ISBN: 9798861890977

CONTENTS

PROLOGUE

Our story begins with a very tough, very old, old lady. This old lady was called Francis and she had been caught not once, not twice, but three times stealing tins of mushy peas from her local Aldi. All three times she had been heavily scolded and gotten away with just a small fine, but on this particular day she was on her last warning; one more time and poor Francis would have to serve time in jail for it. However, she was confident that she could get her hands on those mushy peas without getting caught. After all, she had only been caught three out of one thousand, one hundred and twenty-eight times.

Sadly for Francis, though, the security guard at Aldi had been shown her photo before his shift so he was already suspicious, even before her recent arthritis caused her to drop the noisy tin of mushy peas on the floor. She was cursing herself and her butterfingers as the police car arrived and she was handcuffed and sentenced to three months in jail for persistent petty crime despite warning.

However, Francis lived in a little village called

Stroganoff and though this tough nut of an old lady was more than a bit strange, the people of the town loved the 85-year-old and when they heard that their favorite old lady was being jailed, well, they were appalled, she didn't deserve that!

It was Francis' bridge partner from the local club that had the idea. Sure, hadn't she seen them at it on the news only yesterday. They'd hold a protest, that's what they'd do. Mary roped in pretty much everyone in the village and together they stormed out onto the streets, waving placards with shouts of "Justice for Francis!" and "Old but Gold!" Mary led the mob, her fat frame jiggling left and right with every step as they approached the police station where Francis was being held, their chants getting louder.

Francis heard distant chants of "Francis! Francis!" as she sat in the dark waiting room at the station and put her head in her hands. She should have known that they'd come. She loved everyone out there, but she wished that they would just get on with their own lives rather than trying to fix hers. She did smile a little though as she saw the policewoman at the desk huff and make her way outside to tell them to back off. She heard increasingly loud shouts and wondered how long they would hold out. In her experience, her friends didn't give up.

For two days and nights the riot went on, whole families, from toddlers to grannies stood in the rain shouting and roaring, ignoring the police's outcries. Until finally, early in the morning on the third day, just as the villagers were beginning to lose hope, the Chief of Police stood in front of the crowd and after about a quarter of an hour spent attempting to gain silence he began to speak.

"We have come to a decision," the burly man in uniform announced, "Thanks to your protests," a cheer went up, at which the policeman frowned, "we shall give Francis a choice." The crowd hushed. "She may go through with her earlier sentence, *or* she may instead choose to spend the year in a small cottage in a hill which is very peaceful and which the police force use for mental health recovery. I sincerely hope that you are happy, because, frankly, that is all you will be getting."

Of course, there were shouts of "Just because she's old doesn't mean she's a loony!" and "Our Francis doesn't need to go to an asylum!" but the policeman just turned on his heel and walked back inside. There he looked down at Francis who sat up in her chair in his presence. He explained the choice that she now had to make. The old lady pinched her nose, why hadn't they left well enough alone?

Though it was the absolute last thing she wanted to do, she agreed to go and live in the country retreat, for the sake of the protesters. She was not at all happy as the police car pulled up to take her away.

1.OLD LADY ON THE LOOSE!

"It was only a coupl'a tins o' mushy peas and they're sendin' me to live in a bloody hobbit hole, I swear to God!"

It had been a long drive to the cottage and to Francis, it certainly wasn't worth it. When the police had referred to the house as 'in a hill' they really hadn't been joking.

It reminded her of The Lord of the Rings actually. It was a tiny cottage set into the side of a small hill in the rolling fields surrounding her. There were three pretty flowerpots on either side of the small, round, door which were perfectly symmetrical. Only a portion of the front of the house was revealed and it was painted a bland cream. It looked as if the house had belonged to someone with slight OCD, or so Francis thought, *"Livin' in this ol' hole in the ground at my age, that's not good fer my health, sure, tis not meant for people, tis meant*

4

for hobbits, I'm tellin' ya! I know they meant well an' all but I think I woulda' rathered jail, I coulda' made friends with people with names like 'I'm not tellin' you, you ol' scumbag'*, it could have been fun, but instead I'm stuck in some country sanctuary ting, I'm tellin' you…..."*

As soon as Francis had seen the house, she hated it so much, she knew that she wouldn't give in without a fight. And so, she fought and fought as the Chief of Police struggled to move her from the car up the gravel path to the round, bright red door of the cottage, his face pink with the effort, wishing that his useless assistant would help him out with the violently kicking and screaming old lady rather than just standing off with his eyes glazed over, head in the clouds. Francis screeched as she was pulled out of the car and up the gravel path at a snail's pace.

In his mind's eye, the police assistant, Jim, had just realized he'd won the Lotto, and he was booking a two-month holiday to the Caribbean, in a 5-star hotel, with an all- you-can-eat breakfast buffet. He was still at the travel agents when he felt a big brown boot kick him in the shoulder, he looked up angrily and was about to shout when he saw the Chief's face and thought that maybe, for the sake of his job, he'd better go back to being low-wage Jim and help.

The fight went on and on and over her shouts the Chief explained to Francis that on exceptionally good behavior, she may be let out in nine months, or even sooner, though personally, and he kept this to himself, he thought that the chances of any good behavior from the old lady were equal to the chances of pigs flying.

They continued to make extremely slow progress towards the door with the handcuffed old lady, however, proceedings were a little faster with the assistant now helping and eventually, about an hour after the door of the car had been opened, the old lady was dragged right up to the door. On closer inspection, she realized that the paint was peeling,

"An ol' dump of a place" Francis thought as she attempted to bite the Chief's hand, who slapped her in the face. She yelled.

"Yes!" exclaimed the exhausted man in delight as he reached the house "We got her! Just keep a hold of her there while I unlock the door" he shouted to his assistant "She's handcuffed, so she can't do anything to you."

He shoved the flailing old lady into his assistant's arms and began to reach into his pocket for a ring of silver keys. He turned around and began to fiddle around with them for a bit, trying different keys in the lock attempting to find the correct one. The more he tried to rush, the more the keys seemed to slide through his fingers. In the beginning, he could hear screaming in the background from the old lady, but it later became silent. He assumed Jim had muffled her. About a minute later, he found the key that opened the door. It swung open and he turned around to face Jim and Francis triumphantly.

Only it was not Jim *and* Francis he saw; it was only Jim. Jim with his eyes glazed over, Jim in Lottery-land and Jim with a pair of unlocked handcuffs lying on the gravel in front of him. The clueless assistant didn't even notice the eyes on him. The Chief took a deep breath as he scanned the fields surrounding the cottage. Nothing. He looked in the car. Nothing. He slammed the door and turned to face Jim.

"Sorry, wha-?" Jim blinked slowly.

"Well...where is she?" The Chief's hopes weren't high, but he decided to ask anyway.

"Who- ohhhhh...her. Em..." Jim looked to the floor.

"Francis O' Leary - Location unknown. Over" the Chief murmured into his walkie-talkie. Then he spoke aloud, "In the car, Jim."

Jim went to get into the passenger seat, but his superior pulled him back.

"In the back," he said firmly. Jim hung his head and sloped into the back of the car, embarrassed. He was in for it now.

*

"I can't believe you lost a frail old lady. I mean, SHE'S 85!" The Superintendent's face was bright red as he roared at Jim Rose, *former* police assistant.

Jim mumbled something under his breath. It had been a couple of hours since he had arrived back, and he had been brought straight to the Superintendent's office. He now stood before the plump, red-faced man, shaking. He stared down at the coffee stain on the floor, trying not to look his boss in the eye.

"What's that?! You're sorry, is it?! Well, at this stage Jim, it's just not good enough. Straight from the day you walked in here and spilt my coffee all over the place, I knew you were trouble. And look me in the eye when I'm speaking to you! Thank you." The Superintendent rubbed his nose and made a hrumm noise. He seemed tired. "Jim, I'm sorry, but this is getting ridiculous. Do you have anything to say for yourself?"

Jim blinked.

"Er, I will get better sir." he murmured quietly, "I'm sorry for losing Francis sir."

"Sorry?!Don't say sorry to me! Say sorry to the Chief. From what I've heard, he'd spent half the day fighting with her and then handed her to you for sixty seconds and you lost her! I can't believe it Jim, I really can't."

Jim stared down at the floor again.

"Well, Jim, I am sincerely sorry, but, as I have seen zero commitment from you since the moment you walked in here and now you have lost one of our most important captives, with no excuse but the fact that you were daydreaming, I'm going to have to say that, for now, it's the end of the line for you here. So, thanks but no thanks Jim. You're fired."

Jim seemed to shrink away to nothing as he thanked the Superintendent, not meeting his gaze again and backed out of the door hurriedly. His shoulders drooped as soon as he left the room and he miserably sloped down the pale blue painted corridor towards the lockers where the lower ranking police left their things.

When he arrived at the grey metal lockers, he began carefully placing his things into his bag. One by one, he took out his mug, his folder, and his badge. He looked at it sadly before dumping it in the rubbish bin in the corridor. He quickly took the rest of his things and briskly walked out through the lobby to the car park. Then he remembered his mom was meant to collect him after work today and his chin drooped even further. He sat on the wall and slowly took his packed lunch from his bag and began to eat. He would have to wait a while.

Meanwhile, posters were being pinned to lamp posts, articles were being typed and news items were being scripted as Francis ran further and further away from Stroganoff.

Further and further away from her home.

2. ON THE RUN

Francis panted and began to slow down. She'd spent the last day running as hard as her thin, wrinkly legs would go and now she felt like she could just collapse. And she was tempted to do just that. She had noticed that the assistant was a wimp and had taken her opportunity to get away, using the little tricks she had up her sleeve.

She had ran out through the fields until the house was well out of sight and had later reached a narrow, winding, country road. She didn't know where it led, but she did know that she was getting further away from the police, which was good. The light was now fading fast, and she was beginning to wish she was at home watching Tipping Point in her tartan slippers rather than out here in the rapidly decreasing temperatures.

She had been walking for a while in the

dimming light before it came to her that she would need to find somewhere to sleep. But where? She was on her own on a country road and she was sure that she would be wanted by the police so she couldn't just go into any old B&B. Regardless, she had no money to spend there.

She walked and walked, pondering where she was going to sleep, not coming across anything, until she was forced to acknowledge the growing darkness and the fact that she would *have* to sleep somewhere. She began to worry. She went on and on, until the sky was so blackened that she couldn't see in front of her. That was when she saw the neon lights of Aldi ahead. She knew it was near closing time, so she picked up her pace again to make it to her favorite place and get some mushy peas before it shut its doors, otherwise she wouldn't eat for the night.

So, she got out her Specialbuys magazine and walked casually towards the eerily quiet Aldi. After doing her thing she walked out satisfied. She cracked open her green tin of peas and began to eat them raw(as she usually did) as she sat down on the wall outside the shop. She yawned. Despite the temporary distraction, she still needed to sleep, and she still didn't know where.

That was when she saw an old ruin in the distance. It seemed like a fallen-in castle of some sort, but Francis was feeling pretty hopeless, and her wrinkled old face lit up at the sign of a building she could stay in. She didn't seem to notice, or care about the crumbling walls of the place as she jumped up, abandoning the peas and began to hum a cheerful tune from her days in the church choir as she made her way up the long, winding road through the fields up to the castle.

She was really getting into the song and about halfway up the hill she burst into song,

"Jesus is risen, he has saved his people!" she sang out to the now moonlit hills around her. "Sing out your praises, Hallelujah! Hallelujah, Hallelujah, Hallelujaaaaahhhh, Hallelujah, Hallelujah, Hallelujaaaaaaaaaaaaaaahhhhhhhhhhh!"

To her right a murder of crows scattered from a tree, squawking loudly in horror. She looked up and saw a full moon in the sky shining down on her, bathing the hills in a soft white light, and making the castle look rather eerie. She had never liked full moons. She thought they brought about stupid superstitions. And stupid people.

She was nearly at the castle now and she could see an information board ahead of her. She didn't stop to read, but she could see from where she was that it said something about an old king of Ireland. She didn't care. The desperation had made her slightly delirious, and she saw in her mind's eye a comfortable house. She thought about how they might have garden peas there, for a change from the mushy peas (despite her deep love of the canned delicacy, sometimes enough is enough).

The castle was now just one or two hundred metres away and Francis was excited. Her imagination was getting a little carried away. Maybe they'd have heating, and she could warm her bum on the radiator. Maybe they'd be able to give her a cup of tea, even. Her heart was racing as she stepped up to the castle, just a dark shadow now.

Though the castle was only any good for tourists nowadays, as Francis stepped up to the massive, rotting wooden doors and banged the rusting door knocker so aggressively that some of the peeling paint fell off, she was gone so crazy with hope that she felt confident her knock be answered.

3. A NICE COSY PLACE

No answer. She knocked again. Still nothing. Francis was puzzled. She had kind of lost all sense by now, in her desperation, and found herself outside in the growing cold wondering why no one seemed to live in this *Nice cosy place'.*

She banged on the door again, the old knocker nearly crumbling in her overly firm grip. Still no answer. And again. Nothing.

"Well feck this!" she muttered, as she kicked the door hard, the ripped sole of her boot flapping. The door promptly swung open, creaking, revealing a damp, dark, hallway. The walls were bare stone, and the floor was covered in muck and bird poo. She looked up at the high ceilings, but instead of seeing the crumbling reality, she saw a lovely home, it was just dark at this time of night, she thought.

Francis began to walk in, wondering if she might find a kitchen somewhere in this clearly deserted place and if it could possibly contain some garden peas, even mushy at this stage would still be lovely.

As she walked up the dank corridor, which was almost pitch black, excepting a sliver of moonlight coming from the still ajar door, she stuck her head in each of the open doorways off it, looking for any sign of food. All the rooms contained nothing but the odd mouse that would scuttle across the room, or, in some cases, a crow which would swoop down from the ceiling, barely missing Francis' face as it brushed past.

One time she strode confidently through one of the archways in her battered, nearly falling-apart brown boots and promptly cursed, when she realized she had stuck her head straight through a sticky spider's web, which tangled in her grey hair as its inhabitant crawled over her face. She recoiled quickly and batted the large spider off her long, wrinkly nose and attempted (but failed) to pull the web's strands out of her hair.

Her eyes had now adjusted well enough to the darkness, and she could just about make out the large cracks down the wall. Up until then, she had thought only of her hopes to find peas, but now, as she spotted another dark shape scutter across the floor beneath her, she was beginning to come back to the reality of the situation.

Just as her mind began to stray from peas and she began to worry, she heard raucous squawking from far behind her, quiet enough at first, but getting louder. Initially, she didn't pay much attention, she just kept peeking into rooms, still trying to keep hopeful, but soon, she just had to worry about it.

It was not at all like the soft cawing of the crows and ravens she'd heard earlier. Oh no. Nor the cooing of a pigeon. This sounded like some sort of pterodactyl, and it sounded like it was getting closer and closer to her by the second. It grew louder until she leapt through the nearest door into the next room, still not looking back.

The intensely high-pitched noise got louder and louder and louder from behind her. Francis didn't know what it was, where it was coming from, what to do.

That's when the noise became so ear-piercing, she couldn't stand it. She was just slamming her hands over her ears when she heard a great flapping noise like wings and shortly afterwards, she felt an intense pain like a red-hot poker on the back of her head before her world began to spiral before her eyes.

The room spun and spun around her, rapidly getting bigger and smaller, like a hypnotist's wheel. She felt pain stabbing her again and again and the room began to black out quickly as Francis fell to the hard ground and began to slip away from consciousness, into the darkness that seemed to be swallowing her up like a thick liquid being poured over her, until she was totally consumed by the darkness.

4. SIRENS

Francis blinked rapidly as she looked around the now daylit room as it swam back into focus. Her vision was blurry as she looked around, trying to get up from her uncomfortable position on the cold, hard floor. Daylight seemed to be flooding into the room via an open shaft in the ceiling and she blinked again as she struggled to adjust to the harsh light. She had no memory of this place, confused as she looked around.

That's when she became aware of a stabbing pain on the back of her head, and her back was sore too. '*Sure, this has to be a dream, what am I like, having dreams like this? Sure, I've no reason to be worried!*'

Little did Francis know, she kind of did. The noise that night had been coming from a large kestrel. In fact, not just a large kestrel, but the largest bird of prey for miles around. The locals knew it as the 'Gargoyle' and at a certain time of year, parents wouldn't let their kids outside, for fear of what happened to Francis happening to them. An attack.

'Janey-mac, what's wrong with me?' Francis thought, as she became more and more aware of the pains, the worst being in her head, now spreading down her back. She knew now that this was definitely not a dream. These pains were real as hell and they could have nearly killed any old lady, or at least confined them to their bed.

However, as the title suggests, this particular old lady was very tough, so she just decided to stand up, give her back a loud crack and make her way out of the horrible building as soon as possible. Her body ached all over from lying on the hard floor all that time and she had no idea how long she'd been knocked out for, however, she just got on with it and began to walk down the hill again. As she left, all she knew was a severe pain in her head and back and a *terrible* need for peas.

She walked for ages and ages that day, trying to get as far away from that horrible place as she could, making sure to go in the opposite direction that the signs for Stroganoff were pointing. Only making one quick Aldi pitstop at the first one she came across, she continued walking till dusk.

When it began to get dark again that night, she didn't want to make the same mistake as she had the night before, so she decided to just play it safe and find a bush to sleep in along the winding road she was walking along. So that's what she did. It was far from comfortable, but it did the job, and she got some bit of sleep anyway, if not much.

So, for the next several nights, that's what she did. After walking and stealing from Aldi all day she would then find a spot, in car parks or in hedges, to sleep for the night. One bright morning, about a week after she escaped, she was walking through a small village, and she saw a poster stuck to a lamppost. She wasn't really looking properly, so she presumed that it was just some election candidate or something.

She didn't pass any heed until she saw the same kind of poster again outside a shop down the road and stopped to have a good look. On closer inspection, the face on the poster wasn't just any old could-be town mayor, it was in fact, Francis realized, an extremely bad sketch of someone she thought might be her. Underneath the image, it read:

WANTED: Francis O'Leary (depicted above) for theft. **REWARD:** €5,000

Francis' jaw dropped. I mean, she knew she wouldn't be let away easy, but, five thousand euro, that was a lot of money. She needed to get out of here, fast, and without anyone seeing her. She would have to be more careful from now on, now she knew the police were making a real effort to catch her.

She pulled her knitted beige cardigan over her head and ran through the town and out onto the roads beyond again. For now, at least, it was safer to keep well away from people, she was better off to get looked at strangely all through the town than to run the risk of getting arrested again.

So, deciding it would be safer not to visit Aldi in that particular town, she headed off again, walking down the road on an empty stomach, searching for somewhere to get some much-needed rest. After another hour or so, she found the perfect spot (as bushes go), a lamb's ear shrub, with their silky, slightly fluffy pale green leaves, they made a grand place to sleep.

She nestled down, her makeshift bed was cold but comfortable, she thought, as she drifted off to sleep.

*

It was pitch dark when Francis woke that night, to the sound of a piercing siren in the distance. She sat up, alert. The shock of the wanted sign on the previous day was not forgotten and Francis couldn't help but wonder what the police were doing out here in the middle of nowhere at this time of the night unless someone had recognised her in the town and they were searching for her.

Her breathing unsteady, she knelt up and looked up and down the road cautiously. In the distance, Francis could see flashing red and blue lights, well down the road, moving towards her at a good pace. She reckoned she had about two minutes till the light that was now just a dot was glaring in her face and for Francis, two *years* wouldn't have been enough time.

The sirens got louder and louder as she looked around her in panic and she was so hysterical that it took her three crazed 360° turns just to notice the scraggly row of shrubs behind her. Before diving in, she looked back to see that the car was now much closer to her and was slowing down. Francis could just about make out two policemen in the front of the car before she dove into the prickly hedge.

The thorns of the bush cut her skin as she shuffled around, but she had more important things to worry about. One of the men must have spotted her as the car had stopped completely and the ear-piercing sirens had been silenced. She saw the passenger door of the car open, and a burly man got out. The car was only about fifty meters away from her, so close now that she could even hear the policeman grunt as he slammed the door. He switched on a searchlight and shone it up and down the road. As Francis pushed herself further back into the bush, he signaled to the driver in the car and began to walk down the road towards Francis' hiding spot.

The large man's silhouette was getting closer and closer to the poor old lady with every step, shining his torch in the ditch. He was now so close to the gorse bush concealing Francis that she could even hear his gruff breathing and heavy footsteps.

It seemed like no time until the man was right in front of Francis, so close that Francis could see his bristling leg hairs under the slightly too short crisp navy pants he wore as she peered through the thick hedge, that is, she could see them until she chickened out and put her head down, not allowing herself another peek.

She held her breath as she heard his big black boots crunch on the fallen leaves right in front of her. The old lady, crouched down, head between her legs, stayed completely motionless and silent, barely breathing.

Francis felt the glare of the torch pass over her. Only it didn't pass, it stopped. Her heart very literally skipped a beat. The rough breathing was getting louder, as if the man was bending down to get a better look at whatever he thought he'd seen in the bush. She fought her impulse to squeeze into a tighter ball, knowing that staying still was the best thing she could do.

The breathing got quieter again and Francis thought maybe the policeman had moved on, not seeing anything. She heard a little shuffling then had to purse her lips to stop herself from yelping. A hard kick in the stomach had winded her and now she was struggling to catch her breath without gasping or giving herself away by making a little jump. She managed, just about, to retain steady, almost silent, breathing through her nose and stayed still as well, which in itself was a small miracle.

She heard nothing for a moment and prayed to God that the policeman hadn't heard or seen anything. The light moved away from her, and she allowed herself to exhale through her mouth again. She was still on edge, but she thought maybe the danger had passed.

But then another harsh kick with a hard-toed boot forced her to gasp in alarm.

'*Oh no!*' she thought '*He must have heard me now.*' She stayed still but just about. Fear was taking over as she felt the glare of the torch shine on the top of her head once more. She heard the man curse under his breath and say something like, 'Damned old lady has me working overtime and not a $#%*!&@ sign of 'er'

Then the glare of the torch moved on and she heard his footsteps getting quieter as she watched him walk another bit down the road. She scarcely let herself breathe until the searcher waved at the other man in the car who drove down to him, and the policeman hopped in. As they drove away into the distance, Francis still didn't let herself move. And she didn't move, or sleep, till morning, when she got up and began to walk again, this time with more caution.

She didn't sleep for three more restless nights and brought her Aldi visits down to a minimum. She was really in danger now, and she knew it.

5. THE METHOD

She had the sneaky art of Aldi robbery down to a tee. She strolled into the shop casually, flicking through a Specialbuys magazine, seeming fixated on one item. One day a screwdriver, the next bedclothes. It didn't matter. The magazine was years old anyway so none of the items would still be in stock.

Once past the guard at the door, she would walk through the aisles, towards the middle aisle, casually brushing against the mushy peas on the way. Appearing not to find what she was looking for in the middle aisle, she would make her way out of the shop again, a puzzled expression on her face.

For around thirty years now, no one had noticed her slightly bulging stomach on her way out, or the fact that the magazine she was holding said that the objects were supposed to be in stock from a date years earlier. Her technique was perfect, and she walked out of the remote Ballysagart Aldi she had found feeling exhilarated. Only that feeling reminded her all too much of her home in Stroganoff and coming home from a trip to Aldi that nearly ended in disaster, but just about didn't.

To explain the feeling to people who weren't robbers was nearly impossible, Francis thought. But the closest she'd ever felt to it was when her daughter had convinced her to go on England's fastest rollercoaster. Yes, that was the feeling alright. True exhilaration. But the thought of her daughter brought memories flooding back. Flashbacks. Of a time when she never stole anything and wasn't tough in the slightest. A time when she was just a regular lady.

6. MANY YEARS AGO...

"Catriona, I swear, you're going to be late!" shouted a much younger Francis up the stairs "Your dad is waiting, you'd better hurry on!" A young girl came rushing down the stairs, taking it two steps at a time, Francis' eleven-year-old daughter, Catriona. She was giddy with excitement at the thought of going camping with her dad.

"Coming, coming!"

Her mom had shuddered at the thought of going camping in the *wilderness,* so her and her dad would head off by themselves, just the two of them. The car boot was packed with gas rings, sleeping bags, pots and pans, camping chairs and of course, taking up most of the space, their tent.

"Love you, Mom!" squealed Catriona excitedly as she gave her mom a tight hug.

"Love you too honey, have a great time" smiled Francis as Catriona hopped in the passenger seat of the car "Bye Jamie!" she called out to her husband as he backed out of their driveway. She watched the car as it got smaller and smaller, eventually disappearing into the distance.

Once she could see no more of their bright red Mini Cooper and there was nothing more to see outside, she went back into the house and began to complete the series of household chores she had to do before she could relax. She only had an hour before her favorite TVshow started so she rushed around the house, hoovering, ironing, dressing beds, etc.

All the time she wondered where her family were now, what they were talking about at each moment. Maybe they'd be imitating the stupid radio show they always listened to together, or wondering what adventures they'd have camping.

Finally, her chores were finished, and she could sit down to watch the latest episode of her favorite show except for Love Island, in her opinion the best show ever, Keeping Up With the Kardashians. She loved it. So much drama. She was just settling down on the coach, getting comfy, when the landline rang. She groaned, but got up to answer the phone, after pausing the telly.

She picked up the receiver and heard a deep voice introduce himself as the Chief of Police. He went on and on telling her how this was the number they had had on file for her but weren't sure whether it was still valid and didn't know.... All of this time Francis was just waiting to see why she'd been called, holding her breath and praying it wouldn't be anything bad. However, it was.

"The roads were very icy on the cliffs which your husband and daughter were driving across this morning." The policeman explained "And the visibility was low. We believe their car must have swerved off the road at some point. The drop was very severe and when we were alerted, we arrived on the scene to find that both your husband and your daughter had suffered fatal injuries when the car crashed on the rocks. They had unfortunately both passed away from blood loss by the time we reached them. I am so, so sorry Francis, but sadly, as they were in a very remote area, no ambulances could reach them in time to help. Did you get all that Francis?" there was a long pause "Did you get that Francis?"

"Yes" said Francis, in between the sobs that had started.

"I'm so, so sorry Ma'am. Later today, you will receive a call which will go into further detail about the incident. Have a think and if you have any questions, you can ask then."

Francis could barely hear him over her own sobs. Halfway through his next sentence she slammed the receiver down, her whole body heaving with sobs. She threw herself down on the couch and buried her head in a cushion, weeping.

Weeping for her almost perfect life that she had just lost. Tears streamed down her face. She felt as if she'd been punched in the gut and she cried like she'd never cried before.

All day she went on like that, crying and crying, feeling like she'd never care about anything ever again. As the day went on, she went from pain, to anger, to guilt, all the time crying, quiet weeping to huge, racking sobs. She felt so hopeless. She didn't eat for hours and hours and didn't move from the couch either.

Hours after the initial phone call, it was dark outside by the time the phone rang again. She jumped. She remembered something some man had mentioned about a second call, but she couldn't remember what. Most of the information she received on that horrible call had gone right in one ear and out the other, all she knew was that they were dead. Her family, her everything. She got through the phone call by just staying silent and resisting hanging up, not really registering anything he said, just crying silently to herself for a good half hour, she caught a few words, like bodies and tragic and, of course, she heard the words 'I'm so, so sorry' again and again.

Once she had hung up the phone, she suddenly noticed how hungry she was and searched around for something. She didn't feel like cooking and nothing seemed appealing to her except a giant chocolate bar she'd gotten for her recent Birthday, so she ate the whole of that in about five minutes before she noticed the darkness outside and she dragged herself upstairs and into bed.

Just as she was climbing into her bed, she caught a glimpse of herself in the mirror, and she looked terrible. Face red and tearstained, her brown hair all over the place, tangled and messy. And worse still, she had chocolate smeared all around her mouth. It made her angry to see herself like that. Only this morning her hair had been curled and pristine and she had had her make-up done nicely. Now she was a mess. An utter mess. And as she lay in bed trying to get to sleep, she decided that she couldn't let herself become this, she couldn't.

So, in the stage between awake and asleep that night she thought *'I'm all alone now. I've got no one. But,'* she decided *'I won't let it get me down. I won't cry, I won't lose myself,'* she promised, pulling herself up on her elbows in bed, speaking aloud now, wiping away the last tear with determination only Francis could have.

"I won't give in."

7. EMILY?

When Francis woke the next morning, she remembered the promise she had made to herself all those years ago and decided to do her level best to disregard the horrible pains in her back and head. Disregard the fact that she was living off mushy peas and the fact that she no longer slept on a cozy mattress but in a bush. She decided to just get on with it.

Her friends back in the village of Stroganoff had been like a second family to her. She remembered the time when Mary, her bridge partner and Josephine, the leader of the *Knit 4 India* group had thrown her a surprise birthday party for her sixtieth and had tried to play pin the tail on the donkey. They'd all ended up crashing into the wall, sticking pins in themselves and wetting themselves laughing.

Now that she no longer had her friends, the people who made her life worth living, the only reason she kept going was the hope that someday, maybe, she might be able to go back to

Stroganoff and see them again, though Francis thought that this would probably never be possible.

She eventually heaved herself up out of the thorny bush, groaning and moaning about her aches and pains, but getting up in the end. She sighed. It was hard being an old lady on the run. Anyway, that day she walked for hours and hours, her back was killing her, but she tried to take no notice.

It was dusk by the time she stumbled across a lovely little town. She still hadn't eaten anything that day and she was starving, so the aromas of delicious food coming from the many restaurants made her mouth water and her stomach groan. She wished she had even enough money just to get herself a hot meal. It had been weeks since she'd eaten anything except cold mushy peas.

This small village reminded her somehow of Stroganoff. The people seemed rather chatty and kind. And the village had its own XL Aldi, can you believe it? It seemed the perfect spot. The place was fairly quiet now as it was late in the evening, but a few pubs and restaurants were still open, and they were hopping, some with live music, others with karaoke.

She was even hungrier now after seeing all the delicious pub burgers and chicken wings on tables, so she decided to head for the bright lights of Aldi for her favorite snack, a tin of mushy peas. Once she had gotten the peas without being arrested, she gobbled them down greedily, finishing the can quickly.

Once she was finished and had thrown away the can, she decided to find a place to sleep, which in this case was a couple of particularly squishy garbage bags around the back of Aldi. They stank, but so did Francis, so she barely noticed the difference.

She fell asleep that night wishing that she could become part of a family again, and thinking of how amazing it would be if she could.

*

'No, it's not. It couldn't be, could it?! It's not!' but she knew it was. After a long night of loud rubbish trucks and screaming teenagers, these were her thoughts as she sat on a bench scrutinizing a young family sitting in a café, her heart in her mouth.

Francis' husband Jamie had had a niece who used to be over at their house a lot, a niece called Emily. After the death of her family, Francis had had a fight with Emily's parents, and she hadn't seen her niece in around forty years. Francis estimated that Emily had been five last time she'd seen her, but she was so very sure right now that, unless she was very much mistaken, this was her, this was Emily.

She couldn't be sure of course. The last time she'd seen Emily she was a carefree young girl, now she looked like a careworn mother. But Francis was sure there was a massive resemblance between the two, and she would be very surprised if it wasn't her.

Emily had long, fair hair and beautiful brown eyes and she had two little girls and a tall man in tow, sitting at the table with her. One of the girls reminded her of her own Catriona, at around eleven years old, Francis guessed and the other was a little younger and with darker hair.

The man looked like he was someone on an aftershave ad, Francis thought *'Tall, Dark and Handsome'* she noted.

Francis knew it was her, she was sure of it, it was the look in her eye that Francis thought looked so much like the little girl who used to play in her backyard. So she, allowing herself barely a moment to think, ran up to who she was sure was her niece.

Just as she was about to approach her long lost niece, she stopped, suddenly timid. Herself and Emily had been the best of friends, but Francis and Emily's parents had had a fight and had grown to hate one another. Now, our more than slightly nervous old lady was beginning to have second thoughts. Emily looked so happy with her family, and for a moment, this stubborn old dear considered just leaving the hare sit (and Francis had always been a hare stander).

But then she thought of her dream of being part of a family again.

'Hump this, I'm going up to her' thought Francis *'I always hated indecisive people.'*

And so she decided to go ahead with her plans and, for the first time in forty years, approach her niece.

"Emily?"

8. STUNNED, BAFFLED, CONFUSED AND GOBSMACKED

Francis' voice shook as she spoke, in a quiet, timid voice. The woman gave a slight jump at the sound of her voice and turned around sharply.

"I'm sorry, who are you?"

"Francis? Your aunt? Emmy, you remember me, don't you love?" Francis felt hopeless.

"No." Emily's jaw dropped in shock "Jamie's… it couldn't be…. Not after all these years. No, it couldn't be." Emily looked back at her family and said something quietly to her husband. *'Even more handsome when he's confused,'* thought Francis as her niece's husband whispered something to the kids and they began to walk off.

"After all this time… my parents… if they knew! How did you find me?" Emily asked, looking bewildered "How did you know me, the last time we met I was about five! And what happened to you? You look like you slept in a wheelie bin! How? Just how Francis, how?"

Emily had started off slow, but had sped up into a torrent of questions and Francis was left stunned. The old lady had enough experience to know that this situation needed a good cup of tea and a good, long explanation. So they headed for Emily's house, for Francis to do some explaining.

*

And that's how I ended up here wherever we are, looking like-" Francis looked down at her filthy self and grimaced "this".

Francis had poured out everything, the day she'd gotten caught stealing, her escape from the police, how she'd been attacked by something in the castle, how she'd nearly been caught again, how she'd seen a wanted sign for herself, and how she'd eventually ended up where she was now.

"Well, that was... something." Emily sat across from Francis at her kitchen table in her Barbie-littered living room. Despite the mess, it was a pleasant home and it really looked lived-in. Telling someone all that had happened to her was a relief to Francis and it felt as though a weight had been lifted off her shoulders.

When she had arrived at the house, Emily had started bustling around the kitchen, muttering under her breath.

"She always liked mushy peas, didn't she? Or was that Aunt Margaret?" she said to herself as she pulled a green tin out of the back of the cupboard, it was clear that it was the place they put stuff they never used, as she had to blow dust off the can before cracking it into a small saucepan and putting it on the hob. Then she filled the kettle with water and put it to boil.

Francis sat at the table in silence, staring into space. She was thinking about her memories of Emily when she was small. She was back in her back garden with Jamie, watching Emily as she slid down the small slide Catriona still had from when she was a baby, she was squealing, and Jamie was laughing at her. Then he ran over to her at the bottom of the slide and started tickling her like crazy. Emily was laughing so hard. Francis was snapped out of these thoughts when she saw Emily coming over to her with a large bowl of mushy peas and two cups of tea. She jumped.

"Did I get it right?" Emily asked, somewhat nervously "You like mushy peas, right?"

"Yes, of course."

"Good, now how in the name of Jesus-"

"-I'll explain." Francis replied and she had launched into the story, and now that she was finished, they were both sitting there in an awkward silence. Emily was stunned, baffled, confused, and gobsmacked by her aunt's story.

Honestly, she thought to herself, she didn't think she had it in her. The only stories she'd ever heard about her portrayed her, in general, as just a very old lady who loved mushy peas. She'd probably be dead by now if she matched that description. Sure, she was old and she did love peas, but she was clearly so much more than that, but she still kept going, which Emily thought was amazing. She remembered her aunt vaguely, as a kind, comforting woman, much gentler than her own parents. But she hadn't seen her since her uncle and cousin died, why hadn't they visited her, a poor, lonely widow living on her own.

"Francis, eh, why haven't I seen you since, well-em..." she grew hesitant, the deaths could still be a touchy subject with Francis. And rightly so.

"Well, you see, me and your parents never really got on and we had a bit of a...em, falling out after Jamie and Catriona died and, well, we haven't been able to keep in touch. It's sad really, how we never connected afterwards." Francis' eyes clouded over, but she blinked back the tears.

"Well, thank you so much for telling me all of this." Emily said, sensing that they probably shouldn't linger on the subject. "I've sent Paul and the kids down to the Aldi to get a few bits, which we were planning on doing this morning anyway so they should be around..." she glanced up at the clock "...twenty minutes. We can fill the time with you explaining how in the name of God you can finish a bowl that size of them *manky* mushy peas."

*

"Hmm...I see" Paul looked decidedly baffled "I do find that mushy peas thing a little disturbing…yes…"

As soon as her family had come back to the house, Emily had taken her husband up to their bedroom and left the kids with Francis (She had rooted out another tin of mushy peas and had told the kids that they could have a pea fight for five minutes, if they helped clean up again before their parents came back down and didn't stain any soft furnishings). She had told her husband everything Francis had told her, and after hearing it again, she found it even more amazing. Paul was discombobulated, completely discombobulated. She couldn't blame him though; she really was a crazy old lady. And the question she had asked him was a big one. A really big one.

Since she heard Francis was in a bad spot, she'd been wondering how Paul would react when she asked him, and she still couldn't figure out what he was thinking. He was pacing at the end of their bed, as he'd been doing since she started talking, a brooding expression on his face.

"Well, yes" he said "I think family should come first. We'll give her a chance."

"Thank you. That's why you'll always be my Paulie Waulie."

Emily gave him a quick peck on the cheek and the pair made their way down the stairs into the kitchen, glancing at each other doubtfully. The girls and Francis had cleaned up the remnants of the pea fight and when they heard the dodgy step on the stairs creak they rushed to the couch and Francis turned on the most appropriate TV show she could find, as the girls nudged each other in delight.

"Hi guys! Did you have a nice time with your aunty Francis?" asked Emily.

"Yes we did Mom!" squealed Melanie and Carrie, looking at each other secretively, giggling.

"Can Franny stay?" asked Carrie, the younger of the two, Francis guessed she was around seven.

"Don't be silly, Carrie" said Francis "An old hag like me couldn't stay in your lovely home. I'd drive your mum and dad crazy."

"Well actually, we had the same idea as Carrie," Emily said, glancing over at Paul to make sure he was ready to do this "Francis, we would love you to stay here with us. We've got a spare room down the hall. It's not amazing, but it'll do the job, but only if you'd like to stay, of course. I mean, maybe you have-" she couldn't finish her sentence. Francis had pulled her into a warm hug, muffling her voice.

"I would love to." said Francis slowly and happily as she gave her niece a squeeze. Francis would never *not* be very old again, but she found that, as she hugged Emily, the tough seemed to be melted out of her. It was as if all the built-up pressures she had had inside of her had been released. As though a floodgate had been opened. She just needed to make sure of one thing, before she let her overwhelming happiness take over.

"You're taking a risk, what with the police and that, you know?" she asked. Emily nodded. "And he knows about my, ahem, criminal record" she made air quotes around the words criminal record, as if someone had just made it up that she'd stolen from Aldi.

"Yes, he knows." Emily replied, smiling "Unless there's something I don't know." She said, half mockingly, half questioningly.

"Oh, you ain't seen nothing yet." laughed Francis as she hugged her new family.

9. THE PARTY

Francis was, for the first time in many years, putting on make-up. Well, I should really say she was getting on make-up, as she wasn't the one doing the putting-on bit, Melanie and Carrie, her two grandnieces were.

She couldn't believe it herself, but Francis had been staying with the Donoghue's for almost a year now. The time had flown. She felt she'd grown closer and closer to the family as the year went on, especially Melanie and Carrie, as most days she would mind them while Emily and Paul were at work. Emily was the CEO of a small investment fund and Paul worked in a hardware store.

Today was Francis' Birthday, May 7th. All year she had been trying to hide when it was from the family, so they didn't make a fuss, but they had gotten it out of her and they were planning a huge blowout party with all the friends she'd made over the year. Francis was very likeable, so that was a lot of people.

They also invited all of Paul's family. Of course they couldn't invite any of her friends from home, in case they aroused suspicion and brought the police on her again, which Francis found hard. They also hadn't invited Emily's parents, in case they sparked an old argument again.

It was probably the right thing to do, herself and Emily had decided over a cup of tea in the café. It could ruin the party if Emily's parents started fighting with Francis again. But the decision left Emily feeling guilty and Francis feeling very worried.

There had been a lot more to their argument than what she told Emily and if they did show up, it could be serious. She hated even thinking about Jordan and Jessica these days. They had made her life hell in the weeks when she was grieving for her family and she knew she shouldn't think such things, but she hated them with passion.

The old lady was worried that if 'the J's', as they called themselves, showed up at her party they would ruin not just a good party, but her whole new life as well. And, just like the McDonalds ad said, she was lovin' it.

Her thoughts were interrupted when she felt some sort of crust, glittery, creamy, neon eyeshadow thing being applied to places on her face where it shouldn't be and decided she should probably put an end to the make-up session and go wherever she was supposed to go when people were putting up 'surprise' decorations for her party.

"Now pets, you did a, eh-" she hesitated as she glanced at herself in the mirror "*lovely* job on my make-up, but I'd better get going now."

The girls looked very pleased with themselves as they admired their handiwork. Francis herself thought she looked like a chav crossed with the naked glittery guy from Trolls, the movie. Then she remembered that she might have to wear this to the party and mulled over the idea for a while, before finally deciding that the girls would be just too disappointed if she washed off the embarrassing facial before the party, so she decided to leave it on.

She was about to get up and walk to the café to get out of the way of the party organizers but then remembered her sparkly makeover and decided to stay put in the house, so she didn't get sniggered at by the entire village.

The evening flew by, Francis reading for the most part, occasionally sneaking downstairs to get a peek at how the party was coming along. It looked so good. The marquee was up, the kitchen was decorated and the caterers had just arrived and were setting up. The party must have cost Emily and Paul a bomb, but through the whole thing, they had never mentioned money, which Francis thought was very good of them, but very embarrassing for her.

At about five o'clock, the many guests started to flood in. There was the butcher from the shop in town, and Francis' new bridge partner Margaret, who she thought was a little weedy, but alright. Nothing compared to her old bridge partner Mary. She shook hands with Paul's parents and kissed the French owner of the café they often visited on the cheek. Francis didn't even know some of the guests, some were Emily and Paul's friends whom she had only met once or twice ever and some were people Emily had said weren't their friends but kind of just had to be invited.

All of the guests then went into the unusually spotless kitchen and tried to look polite as they scrambled to get their hands on some of the canapés, you know, the little mini vol-au-vents and the mini pigs-in-blankets. And let's not forget mini quiches. Margaret, her bridge partner even grabbed a whole platter of her favorite ones and took them back to her seat. Everyone was meeting people they hadn't seen in a long time, and they were all chatting and laughing loudly.

They all smirked or burst out laughing when they saw Francis' makeup but the birthday girl was otherwise very happy. She was having a great time, chatting with her friends, and catching up and she had to say, the vol-au-vents were amazing. By her fifth canapé, she had forgotten all about her old enemies and had stopped worrying, focusing on having a good time with the guests. It really was an epic party.

After the first round of drinks and when all the mini versions of food were gone, the caterers said they were ready for dinner. Emily, Francis and Paul (who had turned out to be more than just Tall, Dark and Handsome but really nice too!) started to usher the guests from the kitchen out to the marquee to eat. Before long the first groups of people started moving outside and, slowly but surely, all one hundred people made their way out to the marquee, in groups with their friends.

They went inside, into the massive white tent and oohed and awed at all the beautiful gold and black decorations. There were balloons and streamers and confetti, and it really looked beautiful. There, in the centre of it all, surrounded by bright green balloons, was an amazing three-tier cake, with a sugar craft can of mushy peas on the top. The cake was a mushy pea green and looked like nothing Francis had ever seen before. She gave Emily a massive hug when she saw it and squealed like a little kid in excitement.

Everyone was chatting and having the craic but, in the end, everyone comes to parties for the food and the guests were getting a little peckish. Francis was having a great time having the laughs with her friends and taking selfies but, after a while, she too felt her stomach beginning to rumble in response to the lovely aromas coming from the kitchen.

Everyone was happy when finally, the first waiter came out, balancing plates of delicious smelling food on her arms. Each meal consisted of either beef or chicken, mash, carrots, and gravy. And let's not forget the most important part of the meal, a large helping of mushy peas.

Everyone was just about to dig in, forks poised in the air when "Eeagh!" a sharp, high-pitched scream filled the air. There was a clatter and then complete silence.

10. LUMINOUS GYMWEAR

Francis was the first to look and what she saw was exactly what she'd been dreading. An elderly couple in luminous gym wear.

"Oops!" said Jordan sarcastically, smiling in the most fake way possible.

"We are oh so clumsy, aren't we Jordan?" said Jessica even more sarcastically. After all, they had won the International Sarcasm Championships twenty-seven years in a row.

The guests looked around in surprise and saw something strange. Jordan and Jessica, a couple in their late sixties, wearing matching hot pink and baby blue tracksuits with silver strips down the sides. The man's grey hair looked as if he'd slicked it back with a bucket full of gel and the woman's hair was dyed blonde with grey roots and was pulled back into a super slick ponytail, with a scrunchie to match her tracksuit. In short, they looked like ultra enthusiastic gym coaches with severe mid-life crisis.

The 'J's' were standing over the fallen waitress with smug miles on their faces. The floor was splattered with gravy and the plates she had been holding were in smithereens on the floor.

"Well, when some friends living in these parts told us an old lady had come to live with our daughter, we really should have guessed it was you, shouldn't we Francis?" said Jordan mournfully, as the waitress they had pushed over began to stand up and brush her apron down, looking up at them in disgust.

"And we did!" squealed Jessica in a slightly insane manner. The couple roared in laughter as the guests looked at each other in shock.

"Ahem!" Emily walked into the marquee through the open flap in the tent, holding a beautiful vase, her present for Francis. "This reminds me of the time you showed up at my eighteenth and started-"

"Never mind that!" interrupted Jordan angrily, glaring at Emily, but then adjusting his gaze to stare Francis down instead "The point is, we've got a bone to pick with you Francis."

Jessica stepped forward "We let you off easy when it happened, but the accident of Catriona's death brought it all back." Francis looked down at her peas, groaning. "You're the reason that Emily never had a big brother!"

There was another smash as Francis' beautiful gift fell to the floor and smashed into pieces. Emily screamed.

"What on Earth are you talking about?!" she yelled at her parents, her face had gone from tan to bright red in a matter of seconds.

Paul had begun quietly ushering the guests out of the marquee and back into the house. They all moved slowly, in a group, out of the tent, whispering to each other in hushed voices, looking confused and shocked. Paul didn't know what was going on, but he did know that it couldn't be good as Emily's parents were unbelievable weirdos and thought it was better if the guests stayed out of the way.

"Emily, I'm sorry, you've been so good to me, I just didn't want to-" Francis stopped, unsure of how to go on.

"Mommy! What's happening?" cried Carrie as Paul gently lifted her back to the house.

"But, Francis, you said you just didn't get along. What's going on?" Emily asked, confused and flustered. The J's burst out laughing, rocking from side to side in high-pitched loud laughter. She frowned.

"Oh, Emily, you little child." Emily glared at Jordan as he smiled sarcastically at her "I suppose it's time you know the truth." He continued, in a mock baby voice.

"Five years before you were born, Emily, we had another child, a sweet little baby boy, Jamie.

Named after his uncle. We chose the name before he married you of course." Jessica said, looking at poor Francis with distaste. "He went crazy then, influenced by you, poor man." Francis looked up at her icily. She looked so different from the happy, partying Francis she'd been just a few minutes ago. She looked drained and weak. And the J's were relishing it.

"Yes" Jordan continued "Our beautiful baby boy. So gorgeous, Jamie was. But then one day, Jessy and I had gone out with friends and Francis, Jamie's girlfriend, then, was minding him." Emily was glowering at the three of them. She couldn't believe they had never told her any of this.

"So," Jamie continued, glancing over at Jessica and nodding "*acci-den-ta-lly*" they both said in synchronization, "Francis, when carrying our darling boy down the stairs, fell," he glanced at his wife again and they said annoyingly in sync again "*by accident,*" Jordan went on again "dropping the poor baby down the hard wooden stairs, all the way down onto the cold, hard tiles." Emily gasped.

Jessica wiped her eyes although she didn't seem at all sad really. "After days in ICU, we lost our little Jamie." She said in a put-on choked up voice, trying to look mournful.

"I am so, so sorry," Francis said quietly, in a shaky voice, addressing Emily. "Your parents didn't want you to know, so I didn't feel like it was my decision to tell you. I hated lying to you so much, you were so good to me."

"Yes I was!" Emily screamed. Francis cowered under her "I was *so* good to you. I not only left you stay, but I left you become a part of the family! I took you in when you didn't have a penny!" she yelled "I put a roof over your head and put food on your plate for a year and you treat me like some little kid who doesn't deserve to know the truth. You treated me like dirt!" She gasped for air and averted her gaze to shoot dagger looks at her parents.

"And as for you two" she screeched, red in the face "And as for you two, you $!^@#%! You, my own parents, lied to me about having a brother!? You're a disgrace and you're just horrible. That's just horrible. Out! All of you! Get out of my home! Get out of my marquee that *I* paid for! Get out! Just get out of my life, all of you! And Francis," Emily looked repulsed, "Say your goodbyes. I can't live with a person who lied to me for so long. So, as much as I hate putting the girls through this, goodbye Francis." Emily looked her aunt in the eye "Just goodbye."

"The J's will be back!" announced the highly annoying couple loudly as they turned on their heels and walked out. Jessica flicked her ponytail as she disappeared into the starched white folds of the marquee.

Francis hung her head and without looking up said solemnly to Emily "Goodbye."

*

The wails coming from their house could be heard next door. Melanie and Carrie were sobbing in the hallway, waiting for Francis to come downstairs to say their goodbyes. Paul was with them, and though he had developed quite a soft spot for Francis and he was sad to see the old lady go, he could see his wife's point of view and how they simply could not be together anymore. As Emily was getting changed out of her party dress and pulling on her coat, she had huffed a short version of the story to Paul angrily, before storming out to go find out more about her brother, slamming the door behind her.

Most of the guests had left by now, but a few remained in the kitchen, downing cups of tea and biscuits, talking in hushed voices, wondering what had happened. They'd seen Jordan and Jessica leave the marquee and get out of the house through the kitchen and they'd heard the girls crying but they could only make speculations about what was going on. Then Emily had come through, huffing angrily, taking off her earrings and necklace hurriedly, followed, after a minute, by Francis, looking disheveled.

Francis had gone upstairs to pack her things, but soon realized she didn't need to. She had come with nothing but her Specialbuys magazine and her old outfit from her days on the run and that's what she'd take with her. Anything she had now that she hadn't then, wasn't rightly hers, as she hadn't paid for it.

She came downstairs then, to meet the devastated girls and say goodbye. As she came down the stairs, they were begging Paul for her to stay.

"Does she have to go?" sobbed Melanie, her face red and blotchy from crying.

"I'll go off pocket money for a month...a year! Ple-e-e-ease!" pled a desperate Carrie.

Honestly Francis nearly burst out crying herself just looking at them. This house held memories and these people; they were her family. She'd learnt to take them for granted as much as she had Catriona and Jamie, almost, and now she was losing the people she loved the most, again. Tears threatened to fall, but she held them back.

"I'm sorry girls, and I'm truly sorry to you, Francis, as well" the girls looked around not having realized she'd been coming down the stairs "But it's time to say goodbye."

Francis came down the stairs and kissed and cuddled each of the girls in turn, trying to laugh off how empty she felt inside. Then she looked up at Tall, Dark and Handsome Paul and gave him a hug too, shook his hand and wished him well. She had tears in her eyes as she walked out the door and She was on her own again.

THE VERY TOUGH, VERY OLD, OLD LADY

ACKNOWLEDGEMENTS

Firstly, I would like to thank my amazing classmates in St. Joseph's. You are the reason this book is in your hands right now guys, so thank you.

I would also like to thank my 5th class teacher, Ms. O'Rourke for encouraging me to develop my writing skills and for allowing me to share Francis' story in class.

A huge thank you to my amazing family. A lot of work went into this book and they supported me every step of the way. My sisters were fantastic throughout. Thank you to my mom and dad, for always being there for me.

I am very grateful to Nana and Paddy, who gave a lot of inspiration for this book, and to Eileen, who always encourages me to read.

Thanks also to Nana Curry and Henry, to my godparents, Gavin and Elaine and to my cousins, aunts and uncles, all of whom provided tit bits of inspiration and lots of support.

Finally, most of all, thanks to you, the reader. You are the most important part of this book. Thank you so much for supporting me. And watch out for a sequel, 'cause Francis ain't done yet!

ABOUT THE AUTHOR

Ellie McDonagh is an eleven-year-old author from Cork in Ireland. She lives with her parents, Ray and Maria, her two younger sisters, Lucy and Sarah, two rabbits named Bubble and Squeak and a dog named Penny. She loves writing stories and absolutely HATES mushy peas.

Printed in Great Britain
by Amazon